Cambridge Disco

▶ **INTERACTIV**

Series editor: I

THE SCIENCE
OF DARKNESS

A2⁺

Kathryn O'Dell

CAMBRIDGE
UNIVERSITY PRESS

University Printing House, Cambridge CB2 8BS, United Kingdom

One Liberty Plaza, 20th Floor, New York, NY 10006, USA

477 Williamstown Road, Port Melbourne, VIC 3207, Australia

314–321, 3rd Floor, Plot 3, Splendor Forum, Jasola District Centre, New Delhi – 110025, India

79 Anson Road, #06–04/06, Singapore 079906

Cambridge University Press is part of the University of Cambridge.

It furthers the University's mission by disseminating knowledge in the pursuit of education, learning and research at the highest international levels of excellence.

www.cambridge.org
Information on this title: www.cambridge.org/9781107654938

First published 2014

20 19 18 17 16 15 14 13 12 11 10 9 8 7 6 5

Printed in Dubai by Oriental Press

A catalogue record for this publication is available from the British Library.

Library of Congress Cataloguing in Publication data
O'Dell, Kathryn.
  The science of darkness / Kathryn O'Dell.
    pages cm. -- (Cambridge discovery interactive readers)
  ISBN 978-1-107-65493-8 (pbk. : alk. paper)
  1. Dark energy (Astronomy)--Juvenile literature. 2. Dark matter (Astronomy)--Juvenile literature.
  3. Night--Juvenile literature. 4. English language--Textbooks for foreign speakers.
  5. Readers (Elementary) I. Title.

QB791.3.O44 2013
535--dc23

                                    2013016897

ISBN 978-1-107-65493-8

Additional resources for this publication at www.cambridge.org

Layout services, art direction, book design, and photo research: Q2ABillSMITH GROUP
Editorial services: Hyphen S.A.
Audio production: CityVox, New York
Video production: Q2ABillSMITH GROUP

Contents

Before You Read: Get Ready!

At night the world is dark, but animals and people have found ways of living with darkness.

Complete the sentences with the correct words.

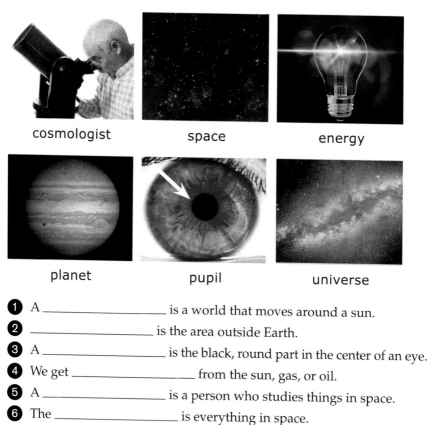

cosmologist   space   energy

planet   pupil   universe

1 A _____ is a world that moves around a sun.

2 _____ is the area outside Earth.

3 A _____ is the black, round part in the center of an eye.

4 We get _____ from the sun, gas, or oil.

5 A _____ is a person who studies things in space.

6 The _____ is everything in space.

Words to Know

Read the definitions. Then complete the paragraph with the correct highlighted words. You can use some words more than once.

explore: go around a place to find out what is there

ground: the part of the earth you stand on

survive: able to live even when things are difficult

smell: know or find something by using your nose

hunt: kill wild animals

adapt: change the way you live

nocturnal: sleeping during the day and awake at night

Madagascar blind snake

Animals, like people, ❶ _____ to the world they live in. Many animals are ❷ _____ – they come out at night to ❸ _____ their world and to ❹ _____ other animals for food. Other animals live under the ❺ _____. The Madagascar blind snake is one example. It can ❻ _____ because it eats insects. It can't see the insects, but it can ❼ _____ them.

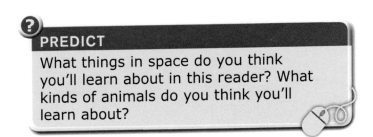

PREDICT

What things in space do you think you'll learn about in this reader? What kinds of animals do you think you'll learn about?

CHAPTER 1

The Dark

WHAT DOES "DARK" MEAN?

Jenny told her roommate Isabel, "Turn on the light. It's dark in here!"

Isabel said. "Why? I like the dark. I like to sit and think in a dark room."

"OK, but we're not living in the Dark Ages,[1]" Jenny said. "So turn on the TV!"

"No, I think people use too much electricity," Isabel said.

"You don't have to be in a dark mood[2] about it," Jenny answered.

"I'm not," Isabel said. "I'm just worried. Are you in the dark about what's going on in the world? We use too much energy! It's terrible."

"I think you worry too much. You have dark circles under your eyes."

[1]**Dark Ages:** a time in the past before modern things were made
[2]**mood:** the way someone feels

"Well, I think it's important." Isabel said.

"I guess you're right, but, actually, I'm afraid of the dark!" Jenny said.

"Afraid of the dark?" Isabel was surprised. "Come on . . . come outside with me."

It was a pitch-dark[3] night. The girls couldn't see in front of them. Finally, they got to the middle of the back yard. "Look up," Isabel said. The sky was completely black except for some stars. "Isn't it amazing?"

"Well, yes, it is kind of beautiful," Jenny said.

The word "dark" is used in many ways in English. It can describe something that doesn't have light. It can mean something is bad or evil.[4] But what is darkness?

---

[3] **pitch-dark:** completely dark
[4] **evil:** very bad

?

UNDERSTAND

Look at the sentences that use "dark" on pages 6 and 7. Can you explain what they mean? Try to use them in other sentences.

CHAPTER 2

Dark Matters

WHAT IS IN THE NIGHT SKY?

Have you ever looked at the sky and thought about darkness? Is it nothing? Or is there something in the dark? **Cosmologists** try to answer questions about things in space. They even study the darkness in space. They say the **universe** is about 5 percent "normal" matter – things we can see, like Earth and other planets, and the sun and other stars. But about 70 percent of the universe is something called **dark energy**. Cosmologists are still studying what dark energy is. They have more questions than answers.

Cosmologists think this dark energy fills space and shows that the universe is expanding.[5] There is more dark energy in the universe now than there was before.

[5]**expand:** get larger

If about 70 percent of the universe is dark energy and about 5 percent is "normal" matter, what is the rest of the universe made of? Cosmologists say the other 25 percent of the universe is dark matter. Dark matter has some weight,[6] it's heavy so we know it's there. But it's invisible, we can't see it. It is very hard to study something that you can't see!

One possible kind of dark matter is a **brown dwarf**. A brown dwarf is too big to be a planet and too small to be a star. Brown dwarfs are colder than stars, and they don't give off light that people can see. Cosmologists found them by using a telescope that finds heat. They found the first brown dwarf in 1995.

A cosmologist uses a telescope to find brown dwarfs.

....
[6]**weight:** how heavy something is

Cosmologists do know a lot about one kind of dark matter – **black holes**. In 1783, English writer and astronomer,[7] John Michell, guessed that there were black holes. He called them "invisible stars." But cosmologists didn't find any black holes until 1971, almost 200 years later. Since then, they've found many black holes in space.

It's very dark in a black hole. There's a lot of gravity[8] there, too. There is so much gravity in a black hole that nothing can get out, not even light. This is why we can't see them. Cosmologists find black holes by looking at things around them. For example, stars and gases near a black hole move very fast.

[7]**astronomer:** someone who studies the stars and planets
[8]**gravity:** an energy that makes things fall toward the Earth

A black hole in space

Black holes can be very big or very small. Cosmologists believe the biggest black hole is as big as ten billion of our suns. They think there is a large black hole at the center of every galaxy.[9] The black hole at the center of Earth's galaxy is called Sagittarius A.

Sagittarius A

Cosmologists believe some black holes are as old as the universe. They think others are made when a large star dies. Our sun is a star, but when it dies, it won't become a black hole. It is not big enough.

Things in space can fall into a black hole, and when they do, they can never get out. But don't worry . . . Earth will never fall into a black hole because there is not one close enough.

....

[9]**galaxy:** a very large group of stars held together in the universe

Video Quest

Wormholes

Watch this video to learn about **wormholes** in space. What don't cosmologists agree on?

CHAPTER 3

Darkness on Earth

WHEN IS IT DARK ON EARTH?

Darkness isn't only in the night sky. There is also darkness on Earth. Usually, it's light in the day and dark at night. But sometimes it can be dark during the day! This happens when there is a **solar eclipse**.

A solar eclipse is when the moon passes between Earth and the sun. The moon's shadow[10] falls on Earth when the moon passes in front of the sun. Sunlight is blocked out,[11] so for a short time it is dark on Earth during the day. Sometimes, only part of the sun is blocked out. Other times, the sun is completely blocked out. This is called a total eclipse of the sun.

[10]**shadow:** a dark area made by something that is stopping light
[11]**block out:** stop something from entering

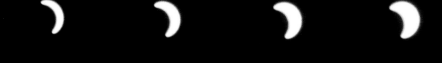

Solar eclipses happen about two times a year. They are seen in different parts of the world at different times as the Earth turns. They last[12] for a few minutes in each place. In 1973, people standing in one place could see a solar eclipse for seven minutes and three seconds. However, scientists could see the eclipse for 74 minutes by following its path on a plane.

It is dangerous to look at a solar eclipse. Because it is dark, the **pupils** of the eyes get very big to let in more light. When the eclipse ends suddenly, the pupils don't have time to get smaller. Too much light can get into the eye. People need to wear special glasses when they look at a solar eclipse.

[12]**last:** happen for a certain time

Oilbirds don't need much light.

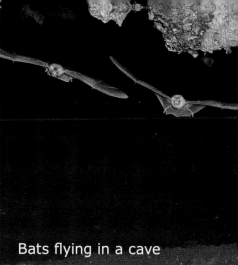

Bats flying in a cave

CHAPTER 4

Living in Darkness

WHAT ANIMALS LIVE IN THE DARK?

Some places on Earth are dark 24 hours a day. Some parts of deep caves don't get any light at all. When people explore the darkest parts of these caves, they wear lights on their heads and carry lights to see. However, there are some animals that are happy to live inside caves. Bats prefer the dark. Most bats sleep in caves during the day, and they don't leave them until it is dark outside.

Oilbirds also sleep in caves. They live in many parts of South America. They make their nests[13] on rocks deep inside caves. Like bats, oilbirds also leave the caves at night. Both animals can live without very much light.

[13] **nest:** a home made by birds

Other animals live in caves all of the time, and they don't need any light to live. Some of these animals are different kinds of spiders and fish. The blind cave fish lives in water in caves. This fish doesn't have any eyes. It is born with eyes, but after three months, skin covers the eyes. The fish doesn't need to see because there is no light in the cave. Hair all over its body helps it find its way around.

Kauai cave wolf spiders live in caves in Hawaii. They are about 2.5 centimeters long, and they look like normal spiders, but they don't have any eyes. They find their way around by using their noses. The cave spider can smell things it wants to eat.

A blind cave fish

A Kauai cave wolf spider

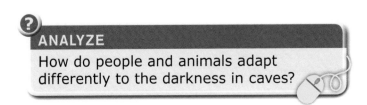

ANALYZE

How do people and animals adapt differently to the darkness in caves?

Many animals, like bats and oilbirds, are **nocturnal**. This means they sleep during the day when it's light, and wake up at night when it's dark to find food.

Nocturnal animals and animals that live in caves all of the time have different ways to "see." While the Kauai spider "sees" by using its nose to smell, bats "see" by using their ears. This is called echolocation. Sound helps them know where things are.

Other animals have special eyes, so they can see well in the dark. Owls are nocturnal. They see well in the dark is because their pupils are very large. They let in more light than the pupils of other animals.

An owl sees well in the dark.

Video Quest

Seeing with Sound

Watch this video to learn about how bats get around. How do they know where things are in the dark?

Another dark place on Earth is deep in the ocean. Sunlight can go up to 1,000 meters through water. The top of the ocean is very bright. Between 200 meters and 1,000 meters there is only a little light. It is like the light we see on Earth in the evening. Below 1,000 meters, the ocean is completely dark. Without light from the sun, it is also very cold deep in the ocean.

Many ocean animals can live in these dark and cold waters. One of these animals is the anglerfish. The females[14] have a thin rod that makes its own light. Other fish come close to the lighted rod, and the anglerfish eats them. The males[15] do not have this light. They stay near the females to survive.

....

[14] **female (noun):** a girl or woman
[15] **male (noun):** a boy or man

An anglerfish uses a rod to make its own light.

CHAPTER 5

Dark Days and Light Nights

WHAT HAPPENS WHEN IT'S OFTEN DARK? WHAT HAPPENS WHEN IT'S NOT DARK ENOUGH?

A dark winter day in Sweden.

Many animals have adapted[16] to the dark. But people don't adapt as easily. In many places, it is dark earlier at night for parts of the year. For example, in Michigan in the United States, it gets dark at about 10:00 p.m. in summer, and at 5:00 p.m. in winter. In other places, this difference is much greater. For example, in parts of Alaska, it is light 24 hours a day in the summer, and it is dark 24 hours a day in the winter. Some people have a hard time with so many hours of darkness. They have a sickness called Seasonal Affective Disorder (SAD). People with SAD do not have much energy. They often feel sad or in a bad mood, and don't want to do much.

[16] **adapt:** change the way you live

SAD affects many millions of people in the world. It is more usual in northern countries like Canada or Finland.

One reason that people get SAD may be because of melatonin. Melatonin is something the body makes to help people and animals sleep. Animals like bears that sleep all winter have a lot of melatonin in their bodies. People's bodies make more melatonin at night than they do during the day. Doctors think that people with SAD do not have the right balance[17] of melatonin in their bodies during the day and night. Perhaps this is what makes them feel tired.

One way to help people with SAD is to use bright lights in homes during the darker parts of the year.

[17]**balance:** not too much or too little

Using bright light for SAD

Other people don't get enough darkness. Scientists say our bodies are made to sleep when it is dark. Before the invention[18] of electricity, people went to bed early because it was too dark to do many things. But today, we live in a world where we can get light any time of the day or night. Stores are open late. Streetlights brighten city streets. We have bright lights in our homes. We watch TV late at night. But people who do not get enough darkness often do not sleep well. They can become sick and feel stressed.[19]

The International Dark-Sky Association (IDA) is a group trying to keep it dark at night. The group started in 1988, and it teaches people why darkness is important.

[18]**invention:** something made for the first time
[19]**stressed:** worried because of something difficult

IDA says we should switch off lights at night to save energy and money (over two billion dollars just in the United States). IDA helps businesses and cities and towns find ways to use less electric light at night.

Not having enough darkness is bad for animals, too. For example, bright lights on beaches confuse[20] sea turtles. Sometimes, they won't lay eggs if it is not dark. The baby turtles also get confused. They use the light of the moon to find the ocean. So they may walk to lighted roads instead of to the ocean.

A sea turtle lays eggs at night.

[20] **confuse:** make something difficult to understand

CHAPTER 6

The Dark Side

WHAT IS A "DARK SIDE"?

In some places, people think of darkness as evil. In books, movies, television shows, and video games the bad character[21] often dresses in black. Cruella de Ville in *101 Dalmatians* wears a black dress and half of her hair is black. In Western movies, which started in the USA in the early 1900s, bad cowboys often wore black hats. In the *Wizard of Oz*, the Wicked Witch of the West is dressed all in black. The most famous example is Darth Vader from the *Star Wars* movies. He wears only black, and he says he is from "the Dark Side," meaning he is bad.

[21] **character:** a person in a movie or a book

Characters in movies are often all good or all bad. This is not usually true of people. Some say that people have "a dark side." This means that people who can be good also have something inside of them that makes them do bad things. Robert Louis Stevenson explored this idea in his book *The Strange Case of Dr. Jekyll and Mr. Hyde*.

Dr. Jekyll is a doctor who wants to separate[22] his good and bad sides to find out more about good and evil. He makes a special drink. When he drinks it, he turns into Mr. Hyde. Mr. Hyde is only evil, and he kills people.

Dr. Jekyll and Mr. Hyde is still popular today. Perhaps this is because people are interested in "the dark side" and understanding what makes a person do bad things.

PARAMOUNT *presents*

Dr. JEKYLL
AND
Mr. HYDE

A ROUBEN MAMOULIAN
PRODUCTION

With FREDRIC **MARCH**

MIRIAM HOPKINS
AND
ROSE HOBART

a *Paramount Picture*

BASED ON THE NOVEL BY
ROBERT LOUIS STEVENSON

....

[22] **separate:** put into different parts

Video Quest

Animal Trappers

Watch this video to learn about restaurant owners that kill and serve wild animals. What animals does the team find? Where do they find them?

CHAPTER 7

What Do You Think?

DO PEOPLE REALLY HAVE A DARK SIDE?

David hunts turtles, and he sells them to a restaurant. The people in the restaurant do not take good care of the turtles. David doesn't know it, but the turtles suffer[23] for days before they are killed for food.

Now, there are fewer turtles where David lives, and one day, they might be completely gone from Earth. There are over 200 different kinds of turtles that are in danger in the world.

Many people say David must have a dark side to kill turtles. They say he must know that it's a bad thing to do.

[23] **suffer:** go through something bad

But David doesn't think he has a dark side. Maybe it's wrong to hurt turtles, but he is just trying to help his family survive. There are not many jobs where David lives. He used to be a fisherman, and he didn't make enough money to pay for his house, food, and clothes for his children. He makes a lot more money hunting and selling turtles.

1. Do you think David has a dark side? Does he have good reasons for why he hunts turtles? Why or why not?

2. Do you think all people have a dark side? Do you think that some things are always wrong?

After You Read

Read the sentences and choose Ⓐ (True) or Ⓑ (False). If the book does not tell you, choose Ⓒ (Doesn't say).

❶ Cosmologists believe dark energy shows that the universe is getting smaller.
Ⓐ True
Ⓑ False
Ⓒ Doesn't say

❷ Cosmologists have found over 200 black holes.
Ⓐ True
Ⓑ False
Ⓒ Doesn't say

Video
❸ Cosmologists believe wormholes join different parts of the universe.
Ⓐ True
Ⓑ False
Ⓒ Doesn't say

❹ In a total eclipse of the sun, only some sunlight is blocked.
Ⓐ True
Ⓑ False
Ⓒ Doesn't say

❺ Kauai cave wolf spiders don't have eyes.
Ⓐ True
Ⓑ False
Ⓒ Doesn't say

❻ Bright lights help all people with SAD.
Ⓐ True
Ⓑ False
Ⓒ Doesn't say

7 Darker skies at night are better for sea turtles.

(A) True

(B) False

(C) Doesn't say

Write

Write an example from the reader for each item.

1 Dark matter _____

2 An animal that lives in the dark all of the time. _____

3 A nocturnal animal _____

4 Something that is better when nights are darker. _____

5 A dark character in a book or movie _____

Challenge

Try to think of your own example for each item.

Choose the Correct Answers

Choose the correct words to complete the paragraph.

You can't see one side of the moon from Earth, not even with a big **1** (telescope/pupil/planet). That is because it is always turned away from Earth. This side of the moon is called "the dark side of the moon" or "the far side of the moon."

Some people have seen the dark side of the moon, but not from our **2** (planet/moon/sun). They have seen it in space. People on Apollo 8 saw it when they went into space to **3** (expand/explore/survive) the moon in 1968. Because the moon is an important part of our **4** (energy/planet/universe), scientists always want to learn more about it. In 2012, a MoonKAM took photos and a video of the dark side of the moon from space.

Answer Key

Words to Know, page 4
1 planet **2** Space **3** pupil **4** energy **5** cosmologist
6 universe

Words to Know, page 5
1 adapt **2** nocturnal **3** explore **4** hunt **5** ground
6 survive **7** smell

Predict, page 5
Answers will vary.

Understand, page 7
Answers will vary.

Video Quest, page 11
Some cosmologists think that one day people could enter wormholes and go back in time or go to the future. Other cosmologists don't think so.

Analyze, page 15
Answers will vary.

Video Quest, page 16
Bats use echolocation to know where things are in the dark.

Video Quest, page 23
They find a turtle in a dark place inside a building and a snake in a box outside in the backyard.

True or False, page 26
1 B **2** C **3** A **4** B **5** A **6** C **7** A

Write, page 27
Answers will vary.

Choose the Correct Answers, page 27
1 telescope **2** planet **3** explore **4** universe